To Oscar

Text, cover, illustrations,
and book design by Stian Hole

Translation by Don Bartlett

First published in Norway © 2010 Cappelen Damm

This edition published in 2012
in agreement with Cappelen Damm
by Eerdmans Books for Young Readers,
an imprint of Wm. B. Eerdmans Publishing Co.
2140 Oak Industrial Dr. NE, Grand Rapids, Michigan 49505
P.O. Box 163, Cambridge CB3 9PU U.K.

www.eerdmans.com/youngreaders

Manufactured at Tien Wah Press, August 2011,
first printing   9 8 7 6 5 4 3 2 1

19 18 17 16 15 14 13 12

Text font Mrs. Eaves

This translation has been published
with the financial support of NORLA.

Library of Congress Cataloging-in-Publication Data

Hole, Stian.
[Garmanns hemmelighet. English]
Garmann's secret / written and illustrated by Stian Hole.
p. cm.
Summary: Garmann makes friends with Johanna, the twin
sister of the girl who torments him at school, when they
discover that they both love adventures and talking about
outer space.
ISBN 978-0-8028-5400-1 (alk. paper)
[1. Friendship — Fiction. 2. Twins — Fiction.
3. Outer space — Fiction. 4. Norway — Fiction.] I. Title.
PZ7.H7072Gar 2012
[E] — dc23
2011022459

Eerdmans Books for Young Readers

Grand Rapids, Michigan • Cambridge, U.K.

"IF YOU BLINK, you're scared of your
mommy," Hannah says, clapping her
hands right in front of Garmann's face.
Garmann blinks, and Hannah cries out,
"Ha! If you blink again, you have to kiss
Johanna." Hannah grins and claps her
hands once more.

Hannah's horrible, Garmann thinks, moving away. He has seen how things work on the playground; he knows that children form a circle around you and shout and jeer. You have to get away before you're left standing in the middle.

For the rest of the break he stays in the shadow of the tree and watches Hannah and Johanna jump rope.

The twins are identical and yet different, Garmann thinks. Johanna is ready to jump in after Hannah. When Hannah starts to move out, Johanna moves in. The girls skip together for a while. But when the rope hits Hannah's legs, Johanna gets the blame. "You're always copying me, you little baby!" Hannah whines.

Johanna gets quiet and walks off.

The twins are at the front of the Constitution Day parade. In front of the band, in front of the mayor and all of the events committee. Hannah and Johanna sparkle. They look like white circus ponies as they march through the school gates, down the main street, and across the square.

"They're like two peas in a pod," Garmann hears some adults whisper as the girls pass by. No, they aren't, Garmann thinks.

Later, after all the holiday games have been played and the last ice cream has been eaten, Garmann feels a hand on his shoulder.

H

e turns and sees Johanna.

"Come on, Garmann, and I'll show you a secret,"
she whispers. Garmann and Johanna head off
through the park, along the wire fence that
Hannah tricked Garmann into licking last winter.
Soon they're by the tall spruce trees. Johanna
looks over her shoulder to make sure no one is
watching them. Then they take the path into the
forest.

"Where are we going?" Garmann whispers.

"Wait and see," Johanna answers.

The path narrows as it enters the dark forest. It's cool and damp beneath the leaves. So many shades of green, Garmann thinks to himself. None of the leaves is quite the same as another. They plunge deeper into the forest, stopping only at an anthill to watch the worker ants carrying spruce needles.

"Wonder how they can tell each other apart," Garmann says.

"I once saw two ants carrying a drop of water between them," Johanna says.

Johanna takes a running start and jumps over a stream. "We're getting close," she says under her breath to Garmann. They creep through the wild brambles. Johanna stops at the edge of a clearing. She pushes some branches to the side and points. Garmann cranes his neck to see.

Between the ferns on the forest floor he sees some twisted chunks of blackened metal.

"You're the only person I've shown this to," Johanna says. "I think it was a space capsule."

"Just imagine it falling on our island, of all islands," Garmann answers in surprise. Johanna cautiously bangs on the scorched metal with her knuckles. Garmann's skin tingles all the way from the top of his little finger down to the graze on his knee. The nice tingle spreads through his body every time his eyes meet Johanna's.

"Do you think there was an astronaut inside? Or two, maybe?"

Johanna shrugs her shoulders and clambers up the tall oak tree. "This can be our secret place."

"Hello, Planet Earth! Everything looks different from up here!" Johanna says with an astronaut voice. She is holding her nose and making the crackling noises you hear in old loudspeakers. "The sky is the sea, and it's full of sea stars!" she laughs. "Come up and look, Garmann!"

G armann is in the mood for fun and joins Johanna in the tree.

"Do you think we can see God out there?" she asks.

"If we're patient, maybe," Garmann answers, pretending to adjust a telescope. "Hello, Planet Earth! This is Comrade Yuri Gagarin, the first man in space. I can't see God up here," he says, disguising his voice.

"Hello, Ground Control here. That's probably because you don't know what you're looking for!" Johanna laughs. "Or maybe God is on vacation. Over and out."

Then the speaker crackles again:

"Do you know that NASA has sent a huge telescope into space? It's called Kepler. The Stamp Man told us. It's going to search for the earth's sister," Garmann says.

"Do you think there's a planet out there just like ours?" Johanna asks.

"Hope not," Garmann says, jumping down from the branch.

"Where have you been all this time?" Mama asks as Garmann slips in through the front door. It's late. Garmann mumbles something about the park and kick the can and gulps down a sandwich.

"Have you got any secrets, Mama?" Garmann asks when his mother comes to say goodnight.

His mother hesitates for a brief second. "Yes, perhaps I have. Everyone has secrets," she says slowly and draws a face in the condensation on the window.

"What about you, Garmann?"

But Garmann doesn't answer. He has closed his eyes and his mind is elsewhere. He thinks of all the things Mama and Daddy don't know. He dreams of Johanna and the space capsule in the woods.

That night Garmann and Johanna float high above the island, so far up that the laws of gravity hardly apply.

Whenever they can sneak away, Garmann and Johanna meet in the forest. There they repair the space capsule.

"Hannah must never know about our secret," Johanna says, passing Garmann some more nails.

"No one in the world can see us here," Garmann answers.

"Do you think someone could see us from the moon?" Johanna asks.

"Only if we stand on the Great Wall of China," Garmann says.

When it rains, water drips through a crack in the spaceship, and Garmann and Johanna snuggle up so they don't get wet. They can sit like that for a long time without speaking. Sometimes they ask each other riddles: "If you say my name, I have disappeared. Who am I?" Garmann says.

All they can hear is the wind rushing through the treetops and a woodpecker a long distance away. Johanna shrugs.

"Silence," Garmann says.

"I know who goes with you to the woods," Hannah says one night when the twins are in bed.

Johanna goes pale. "You're lying," she says.

"No, I'm not. I've seen you," Hannah says.

I know it was you who broke Great-Grandma's glass vase," Johanna whispers after a pause.

At first Hannah is quiet. Then she says, "If you don't tell anyone, I won't either."

"Done," Johanna says. "Now we have a secret too."

IIIne day Johanna and Garmann venture deeper into the forest. Johanna takes off her shoes by a small lake. "Come on! The space capsule is whizzing through the atmosphere! The heat shield is glowing. And it lands in the Atlantic," she says, jumping off the hill.

Garmann closes his eyes and jumps after her. The gray-green water is cool on his skin. The stalks of the water lilies tickle his legs. It's scary and exciting at the same time.

"I can teach you how to swim under water. It's almost like floating in space," Johanna says, showing him what to do.

They see the water striders skating across the shiny surface of the pond by the reeds. "Hannah and I come from the same seed, so everyone thinks we are the same," Johanna says. "But we aren't." The drops of water on her skin disappear one by one in the sun. Johanna looks up and remembers something. "Hannah says if you look into the sun, you go blind."

"Don't believe everything Hannah says," Garmann replies.

"Sometimes Hannah is right," Johanna says.

S itting on a big, smooth rock, Garmann
can feel Johanna's finger on his hand,
and a warm glow passes through his body again.

"Are you good at soccer?" he asks.

"No, I'm pretty bad," she answers.

"Me too," Garmann says. "Are you
scared of growing up?"

Johanna nods.

"Me too," Garmann says.

Garmann looks at Johanna. Her freckles almost disappear when her cheeks go red. They take turns writing words on the other's back with a finger. ASTRONAUT, Garmann writes, and Johanna guesses correctly.

"I have to have the light on when I go to sleep," Johanna says. "You won't tell anyone, will you?"

"I can keep a secret. Cross my heart, hope to die, stick a needle in my eye," Garmann says.

Then it's Garmann's turn to try. "KEPLER?" he guesses. Johanna nods and puts her hand inside his.

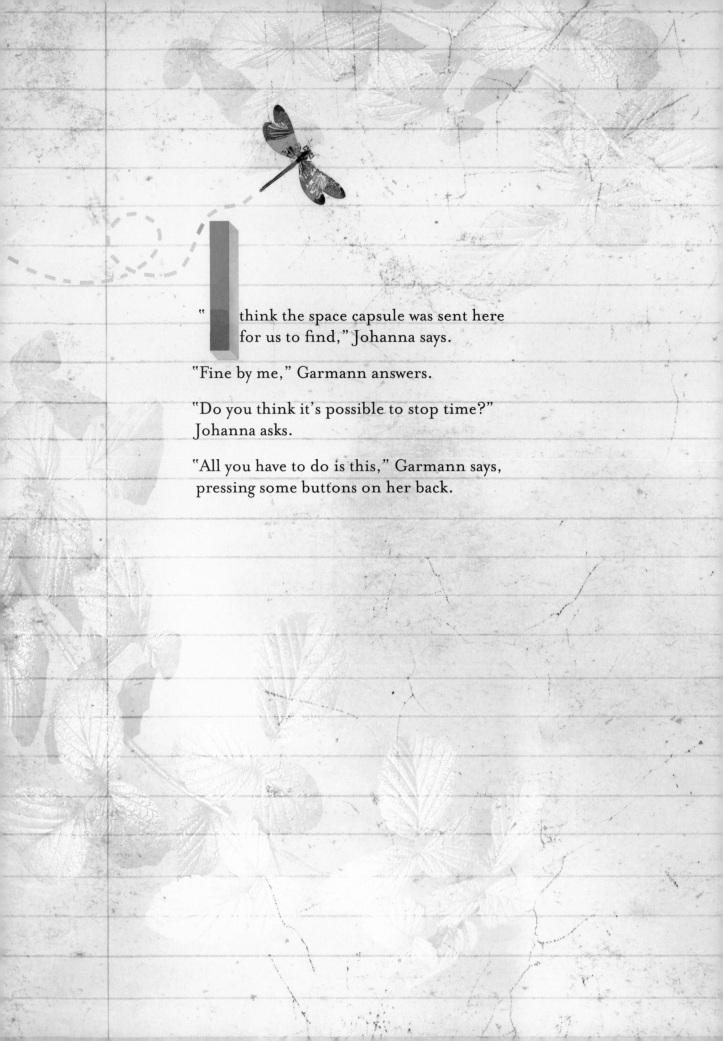

"I think the space capsule was sent here for us to find," Johanna says.

"Fine by me," Garmann answers.

"Do you think it's possible to stop time?" Johanna asks.

"All you have to do is this," Garmann says, pressing some buttons on her back.

"Or this," Johanna answers.